# A Job for Li

by Michèle Dufresl
Illustrated by Cula Carmen Elena

Pioneer Valley Educational Press, Inc.

Santa looked at the elves.
"I need some help," he said.
"We need to make some toys.
Who will help me make the toys?"

"I will help!" said Little Elf.
"I will help you make
the toys!"

"You can't make the toys,"
said Big Elf.
"You are too little!"

"We need to wrap the toys,"
said Santa.
"Who will help me wrap the toys?"

"I will help!" said Little Elf.
"I will help you wrap the toys!"

6

"You can't wrap the toys,"
said Big Elf.
"You are too little!"

"We need to pack the sleigh,"
said Santa.
"Who will help me pack the sleigh?"

"I will help!" said Little Elf.
"I will help you pack the sleigh!"

"You can't pack the sleigh,"
said Big Elf.
"You are too little!"

"I need help driving the sleigh,"
said Santa.
"Who will help me drive the sleigh?"

"I will help," said Big Elf.
"I will help you drive the sleigh!"

Santa looked at Big Elf.
"You are too big," he said.
"You are too big for my sleigh."

Then Santa looked at Little Elf.
"Little Elf, you can help me
drive the sleigh," he said.
"You are not too big."